marie-claude branche

THE TREES KNEEL AT CHRISTMAS

For Public School 77 in Brooklyn

THE TREES KNEEL AT CHRISTMAS

MAUD HART LOVELACE

Illustrated by Marie-Claude Monchaux

ABDO & Daughters Publishing

ABDO & Daughters Publishing
4940 Viking Drive, Suite 622
Edina, Minnesota 55435.

Lovelace, Maud Hart, 1892-1980
The trees kneel at Christmas/Maud Hart Lovelace;
illustrated by Marie-Claude Monchaux.
p.   cm.
Summary: After Grandmother explains why the trees in
Lebanon kneel at Christmas, Afify and Hanna hope to
witness a similar miracle in Brooklyn's Prospect Park.

ISBN 1-56239-999-3
(1. Christmas–Fiction. 2. Miracles--Fiction. 3. Lebanese
Americans–Fiction. 4. Brooklyn (New York, N.Y.)--Fiction.)
I. Monchaux, Marie-Claude, ill. II. Title.
PZ7.L9561Tr 1994
(Fic)–dc20
94-10512
CIP AC

39689 — Ingram 11/94

∞ *FOREWORD* ∞

In the fall of 1949, my mother got a speaking invitation from a public elementary school in Brooklyn, half an hour by train from our home on Long Island.

As the author of the popular Betsy-Tacy books, she got a lot of these invitations, and she accepted as many as she could. But there was a special reason why this one from P.S. 77 was particularly welcome. She wanted to make friends with some Lebanese children, and Brooklyn, which then as now had a thriving Lebanese community, was a good place to find them.

As most readers of the Betsy-Tacy books know, these now-classic stories about growing up in Minnesota in the years before World War I are based on my mother's own girlhood, and the town of Deep Valley, in which most of them are laid, is her home town of Mankato. There was a little colony of Lebanese immigrants on the outskirts of Mankato in those years, and it figures prominently in two of the books: *Betsy and Tacy Go Over the Big Hill* and *Emily of Deep Valley*.

She was doing research for *Emily of Deep Valley* when the invitation from P.S. 77 arrived. So she told the principal that she'd like to get acquainted with a few of the Lebanese students. And after the speech, she met in the library with Annette, Charles, Mary, and Peter, who became her guides.

They took her sightseeing on Atlantic Avenue, the Main Street of Mideastern Brooklyn, with its ethnic restaurants and stores full of baklava and halvah and pistachios, waterpipes and tiny coffee cups and boxes inlaid with mother-of-pearl. They took her to their churches—Greek Orthodox, Roman Catholic, Maronite, Melchite and Syriac. They took her to their homes to meet parents and grandparents who plied her with bread and cheese and coffee and pastries. And one of the grandmothers told her about how in Lebanon, the trees kneel at Christmas.

In an article my mother wrote in 1951 for the *Minnesota Missionary*, the newsletter of the Episcopal Diocese of Minnesota, she recalled that "I immediately wrote down those words, knowing that they could be a title of a book."

" 'Do they kneel in Brooklyn?' I asked."

" 'No.' she answered, shaking her head. 'No one has ever seen them kneel in Brooklyn. People in Brooklyn haven't faith enough.' "

"That lodged in my mind. I couldn't get it out. I began to wish I could write a story about modern children who would try to see the trees kneel in America."

She finished *Emily of Deep Valley* in March of 1950, and somehow couldn't seem to get started on a new Betsy-Tacy book. She still couldn't get those kneeling trees out of her mind.

On August 23, my mother wrote in her diary: "Decided today to write *The Trees Kneel At Christmas*. The theme is faith, and I have faith that I can write it, although I don't know yet the characters, setting or plot."

In December, the story still hadn't taken shape. She was spending more and more time with her Lebanese friends. She went to the Christmas assembly at P.S. 77 and heard the children singing carols and "Rudolph, The Red-Nosed Reindeer". She visited a nearby branch library for the weekly story hour, and there, she wrote in *The Minnesota Missionary*, "I saw my Afify, tucking her little skirts into her ski pants. (I knew her right away). The storyteller, at my request, asked the children to tell him what they thought an angel looked like. When I heard their answers my book began to stir."

On Christmas Eve, my mother and father went to Brooklyn. They drove through Prospect Park and the trees under their blanket of snow. They were welcomed at warm, joyful, reverent Lebanese family parties. They went to a Maronite Midnight Mass with the old lady who had first told my mother about the trees that knelt.

"Driving home early that Christmas morning," she told the *Minnesota Missionary*, "my prayers were answered. *The Trees Kneel at Christmas* came to me just as I wanted to write it. I wrote it in a month."

And now this wonderful story of Brooklyn in 1950 is back in a new edition from a Minnesota publishing family whose roots go back to the Lebanese colony in turn-of-the-century Mankato.

Brooklyn in 1950 was a gentler place than it is in 1994. Even then, it would have been dangerous for two small children to go out alone at midnight. Today it would be unthinkably dangerous, and children like Afify and Hanna would know better than to try. But the streets of Park Slope are still lined with brownstones and buttonwood trees, and statues of animals still stand guard over the Third Street entrance to Prospect Park. Fifth Avenue still blazes with colored lights at Christmas time, and carolers go serenading. And there are families of every race and nationality and faith, as loving and hardworking and devout as the Shehadis.

Readers who remember the original edition of *The Trees Kneel At Christmas* may notice one change in the text. There the Shehadis were Syrians. Here, because the description of the village from which they came to America plainly locates it in what is now Lebanon, they are Lebanese.

Until 1920, Lebanon was part of the Turkish province of Syria. Its people were Syrian nationals, and "Syrians" to most Americans. The Mankato immigrant colony was "Little Syria" to the rest of Mankato. So they were the terms my mother grew up with, and either she didn't realize they needed changing or she didn't want to change them because she thought "Syrian" would still sound more familiar to most Americans than "Lebanese."

But since then, we have all come to know only too well that Lebanon and Syria are different countries, and I'm certain my mother would want to leave no doubt that the Shehadis are Lebanese-Americans.

Merian Lovelace Kirchner
Park Slope, Brooklyn
October, 1994

CONTENTS

CHAPTER

1

Grandmother Begins Her Story

*I*t was the night before Christmas Eve, the most mystical night of the year except for Christmas Eve itself. Some of the solemn joy, the tender hush, the waiting for a holy, wonderful event was already in the air.

In the Shehadi's flat in Brooklyn, the grandmother was telling a story.

"Yes," she said, "the trees kneel at Christmas. Not in this country, though. I've never seen them kneel in Brooklyn."

"But in Lebanon they do?" piped Afify. Lebanon was the country her grandmother came from, and her father and mother, and most of her uncles and aunts. It was far away, across the Atlantic Ocean; they spoke a different language there. Grandmother was speaking it now, but Afify and Hanna understood Arabic as well as they understood English.

Afify spoke English in school, of course. She was in the first grade. And there they called her Mary; for her name was

Mary Afify, and Mary is the same in English as in Arabic. At home, though, they called her Afify (which is pronounced Afeefee). It suited her much better.

She was very small for seven, just a scrap of a girl, with tiny black braids sticking out above her ears. Her black eyes seemed to take up almost half her face. But although she was so small, she was very bright; she was near the top of her class.

She liked to wear a sweater and skirt as the bigger girls did sometimes, and she had persuaded Mother to let her, although her skirt was not much longer than a ruffle, and her sweater looked like a baby's sweater, Mother said.

Afify almost always got her own way. She was very determined. She tried hard not to want to do anything that it wasn't right to do, for if she wanted to do it, she almost always did it.

Whatever she did, she did with her whole heart. That was the way she was listening to Grandmother now. Hanna was playing with his Hopalong Cassidy pistols while he listened, squinting through them, aiming them here and there.

He was only five years old and didn't go to school yet. When he went to school, he would be called John, which was his name in English. He was a round, chubby little boy, with eyes like jet buttons and a rosy, golden skin.

Afify sat on her heels gazing up into Grandmother's

face with eyes that never wavered.

She was thinking about the trees kneeling. She was imagining great tall trees like the ones in Prospect Park getting down to say their prayers as she and Hanna did.

"Oh, I wish I could see them!" she cried. Her high little voice sounded just the way she looked. It chimed like the glass bangles she wore. "Do they really truly kneel?"

"Yes, my heart," Grandmother replied. "They kneel on the Night of the Birth."

"We say Christmas Eve in Brooklyn."

Grandmother nodded. "They kneel on every Christmas Eve."

"No, it is on Epiphany Eve," Uncle Elias interrupted.

He was sitting in his usual corner, short, thin, erect, his right hand on his right knee, his left hand on his left knee, his thin gray hair rising in a curly peak like smoke from a teakettle.

Uncle Elias had bright, mocking eyes and a small mouth that often had a mocking smile. But his lips were folded stubbornly now, and Grandmother's tightened, too. He was her younger brother. He was Great-Uncle Elias, really; but the children called him Uncle. He was the only person who could ever disturb Grandmother out of a cheerful calm.

She was very fat. She sat in a deep soft chair, the back and arms of which were covered with lace that she had made herself. Her cane stood by her side, for she was lame and seldom moved without both her cane and Mother to help her. She always wore a black dress, and thin gold bracelets that clinked as she crocheted.

Her hair was white and her crumpled cheeks were soft. When you hugged her, as the children often did, it was like hugging a soft, sweet pillow. And she always smelled sweet, from attar of roses that she got every year on her birthday—sometimes more than one bottle, for all her children knew she loved it.

She looked up at Uncle Elias, and her big dark eyes that were usually so soft and loving grew angry.

"It was on Christmas Eve," she said.

"Wah!" said Uncle Elias. "You know as well as I do that we didn't make a thing of Christmas in Lebanon. We didn't have a Christmas tree–"

"I like Christmas trees," Hanna interrupted. "We had a Christmas tree last year. I hope we're going to have a Christmas tree this year–"

"Hush, Hanna!" said Afify, although she had been hoping the same thing all day.

Uncle Elias paid no attention to them.

"We didn't hang stockings," he went on. "We didn't even give presents."

"I didn't say we did!" cried Grandmother, flinging up her arms. "I said the trees knelt. Our Blessed Lord was born on Christmas; wasn't He? You don't deny that; do you?"

"I admit that," said Uncle Elias, shrugging his shoulders. "But in Lebanon we considered His true birthday to be the day He was baptized. Then He was born of the spirit, my sister. On Epiphany He was baptized, and on Epiphany Eve He walks toward the Jordan. All the waters of the earth are holy that night because He is about to be immersed. That's why the girls in your story went out to bathe–"

"But Epiphany," Afify put in, "is when the Wise Men came. Was Our Blessed Lord baptized on Epiphany, too?"

"It doesn't matter," said Grandmother. "Do you want

me to tell you this story, or don't you?" She looked at Afify severely but Afify didn't mind. She knew the crossness was really for Uncle Elias.

"Hanna and I both want it. Don't we, Hanna?"

"Sure," said Hanna, cocking both pistols at once. "But I wish Santa Claus was in it."

Uncle Elias had taken him to see a Salvation Army Santa Claus downtown. Hanna had put a penny in his kettle and told him he wanted a sled. He had talked about Santa Claus ever since.

"Please, my Grandmother!" pleaded Afify. "Please! Tell us how the girls went bathing, and threw their clothes on a fig tree—"

"A fig tree!" exploded Uncle Elias. He threw out his hands as though this was more than he could bear. "You are getting old, my sister! The fig tree doesn't kneel, because Our Lord once cursed it. And the mulberry tree doesn't kneel either. It is proud because it can make silk. It was an olive tree the girls threw their clothes on—"

Grandmother began to pound her cane. "It was a fig tree!"

Uncle Elias smiled a superior smile. "It was an olive!"

"I say it was a fig!"

"You may cut off my right arm if it was not an olive."

Their voices were rising, and their *r*'s trilled more and more. They always trilled the letter *r* but not so much as when they were angry.

Afify began to wiggle her loose tooth in her excitement. Hanna jumped up and shot both his pistols and fell dead.

Mother called out from the kitchen where she had spent the afternoon baking Christmas pastries. She had been working on them for several days–shelling nuts, chopping them fine, boiling syrup. Today she had been baking them and the whole flat smelled of their rich goodness, but Afify and Hanna hadn't had a bite yet. They wouldn't be allowed one until Christmas Eve.

"If any trees kneel at Christmas," Mother said, "all of them must kneel. God, the Father, made them all; didn't He?

Just as He made all of us? Maybe you can tell the children the
story after dinner, my Mother. I need Afify to set the table now."

Afify knew that she wanted to stop the argument.
Uncle Elias knew it too, and got up from his chair. He rose
slowly, for he had rheumatism, although he wouldn't admit it.
He liked to act like a young man, an American young man.

He patted his sister on her snowy head and picked up
Afify and swung her around. It was easy to swing her for she
was so small and light. Hanna wanted to be swung but Uncle
Elias said, "O-o-h, no! O-o-h, no!" and backed away. Hanna
was heavy because he was so fat. But Hanna caught him and
hugged him, kicking and squealing with love.

Uncle Elias took Hanna to Prospect Park every day,
and Afify too, when she wasn't in school.

They couldn't go alone, of course. You crossed Sixth
Avenue and Seventh Avenue and Eighth Avenue, as well as
Prospect Park West to get to Prospect Park. These were busy
streets with streetcars and buses and rushing automobiles and
green and red lights to watch out for.

Afify and Hanna did not go many places alone because
Brooklyn is so big. Afify went to school alone, and sometimes
to the corner store for Mother, but nowhere else.

When Uncle Elias put her down she started to set the
table. The dining room was just through an archway from the

parlor. On one side of these two rooms was the kitchen, and on the other were two bedrooms–one for Father and Mother and Hanna; one for Grandmother and Afify–with the bathroom between.

Afify set the table with care. She was proud to be old enough to do it, and tried to make the corners of the cloth hang evenly and to put the knives and forks and spoons in neat, orderly rows.

"I'll be down to hear the story this evening," Uncle Elias said, smiling his disrespectful smile at the door.

Mother went over to him. She was very pretty, with black braids wound around her head and soft dark eyes like Grandmother's. She wasn't fat like Grandmother, though. She was just a little soft and sweet, like a very small pillow.

She put her hand on his arm and smiled into his face. "Do come, dear Uncle Elias," she said. "And let's not have any arguments about the story. Who cares whether it was Epiphany or Christmas, or a fig tree or an olive tree? The important thing is that the trees kneel to worship Our Lord, as all of us should do. And the Night of the Birth is very near now."

"It's tomorrow night!" shouted Hanna.

"Yes, it's tomorrow night. And we should all be loving to each other. Tomorrow night you will be going to midnight Mass–"

"Okeh, okeh," said Uncle Elias, who liked to talk American. He winked at Afify and Hanna, and gave Mother a poke. "I'll behave. No kidding!"

He opened the door, and there was a smell of other people's dinners cooking, and the sound of someone's radio

playing "Rudolph, the Red-Nosed Reindeer." Uncle Elias whis-
tled it briskly as he climbed the dark, narrow stairs.

He lived upstairs with Uncle Charles and Aunt Esther;
Uncle Charles was his son. They were very American. They
had a television set, and Hanna went up to see Hopalong
Cassidy there.

Down one flight lived Uncle
Abdo and Aunt Shafeah. They were
very Lebanese. They smoked
narghiles, which are Lebanese
water pipes. The children called
them hubble-bubble pipes
because of the noise they
made.

Sometimes
Uncle Elias went
down and smoked
one, too. But he
didn't like any-
one to know
it.

The other families in the building weren't Lebanese. They were Italian, mostly, with a few Irish.

"But we're all Americans," Afify's father often said. And he would tell them with wide sweeps of his arm how wonderful America was, with free schools, and people allowed to go to whatever churches they pleased, and elections, so that they could have the kind of government they wanted. No one needed to be afraid of policemen or soldiers, as they were in the old country.

"I'm an American, my Father," Hanna would cry. "I was born in Brooklyn like the Dodgers."

"Yes, my son. And maybe you'll be President of this country some day."

"I was born in Brooklyn, too," Afify would pipe.

"Of course, my little love!" Her father would look at her fondly—at her wispy braids and her shining big black eyes. She wore little blue earrings, for blue is the Virgin Mary's color and it is always well to have a bit of it about you. He would stroke her small, soft arms.

"Of course," he would repeat, "you're an American, too. And America is fine. It's dandy. But the Lebanese girls have very gentle ways. Don't ever forget, my daughter, that your family came from Lebanon!" As though she ever could!

Her grandmother was like all grandmothers, she loved

to tell stories. And Afify loved to listen to them. She liked Grandmother's stories even better than the stories in books. And they were all about Lebanon.

Lebanon was a land out of the Bible, Grandmother said. Solomon's temple had been built from the Cedars of Lebanon. And Grandmother's village had stood in the foothills of those same Lebanon Mountains, looking toward the Mediterranean Sea.

Afify knew just what the village looked like. The small stone houses had flat roofs on which people sat as in a parlor, to talk, or make lace, or smoke narghiles. In the rooms below there were no chairs. People sat on the floor or mats or low benches covered with pillows and carpets.

"Didn't you even sit at a table to *eat*?" Afify had asked.

"Of course. But it was a low table and we sat on the floor beside it. It's a very comfortable way to eat," Grandmother replied. She would laugh. "I was afraid to sit on a chair when I first came to America."

"Did you have beds in Lebanon, my Grandmother?"

"Our beds were like long cushions. In the morning we rolled them up and put them away in cupboards. And another funny thing! In Lebanon we took our shoes off before we came indoors. But the men of the family kept their hats on. In America it is just the opposite. Shoes on and hats off."

Hanna loved that part.

Outside the house, Grandmother said, there were hills covered with flowers, and olive trees full of olives, and fig trees full of figs, and the mulberry trees that Uncle Elias thought were proud because they fed the silkworms.

Down in the city of Beirut there were camels with humps on their backs, and donkeys like the one on which the Blessed Virgin rode. There were bazaars with beautiful things for sale–bright rugs, and silks, and jewels, and perfumes–and pastries like Mother had been baking today.

Some of the very same things could be bought at the Lebanese shops along Atlantic Avenue in Brooklyn.

Strange and thrilling things happened in Lebanon. Saints and angels came in visions. Saints and angels were close in Brooklyn too, of course. Their pictures shared the walls of the flat along with Father and Mother's wedding picture, and a grandfather wearing a small round hat with a tassel, and Afify making her First Communion. An angel hung by a ribbon over Afify's bed, and above that stood Mary, the Virgin, in blue and white robes, a halo about her head, and long golden rays extending from her fingers.

Mary, the Virgin, was as real to Afify as her Grandmother was, and she felt as well acquainted with the Christ Child as with the fat baby in the Giovanni flat.

But there weren't so many miracles in Brooklyn.

Last summer up in Prospect Park she had found a spot that reminded her of Lebanon. There were bushes of white, sweet-smelling flowers, and behind them, making a half circle, three young evergreen trees that gave out a spicy smell.

"Maybe they're Cedars of Lebanon," Afify said.

They weren't very tall. They were tall enough to be mysterious but short enough so that you could feel at home with them. Their lower branches were wide and thick, grow-ing narrower as they went up, and making a peak at the top.

They were set so close together that on one side they shut out the park.

"This is like Lebanon," Afify had told Hanna, smoothing the grass, sniffing the white flowers, and looking up at the friendly little trees.

"No kidding!" answered Hanna, staring. He liked to talk American, as Uncle Elias did.

He looked around, his hands behind him, his small stomach sticking out impressively. "It's a good place for Indians," he remarked.

This was before he had heard about Santa Claus, and he was playing Indians all the time.

"Let's keep it for a little Secret Place. We can call it 'C.P.' for Secret Place. I *think* that secret begins with a C.

It ought to," Afify said.

"Okeh!" Hanna answered.

"Let's not tell Uncle Elias about it."

"Okeh!"

And they never told him. The C.P. was just a little way from the bench where Uncle Elias liked to sit and talk with the pretty young mothers, but the half circle of evergreens shut them from his view.

Sometimes they played they were in Lebanon. And sometimes they played school. And sometimes they played house. And sometimes, to please Hanna, they played Indians.

Afify brought Hubbooba, her doll, and Hanna brought Bobo, an old worn-out bear that he loved more than all his other toys. Hubbooba and Bobo knew about the Secret Place but Uncle Elias didn't. He knew where they were playing but he didn't know it was a secret.

At last he would call, "Hey, kids! Where are you? Time to go home!" And he would start up the slope. But Afify and Hanna would run down before he reached the Secret Place, so that he never saw it.

After Afify started to school, they still came to the park in the afternoons and on Saturdays when Uncle Elias could take them. But in November there was a fall of snow, and then Hanna liked better to go to that hillside where children were sliding. He wanted a sled for Christmas–that was one reason he was so interested in Santa Claus. Afify used to leave him with Uncle Elias and go up to the C.P. alone.

The bushes were bare now, and yellowish brown, but the evergreens were bright as emeralds in a Lebanese bazaar. The snow was soft and fresh for no one else came here except the squirrels that left the tracks of their little feet sometimes. They came even when Afify was there. Fat gray fellows with white undersides, they went frisking up the little trees and sat with their plumy tails erect and quivering behind them, watching her as she made angels.

She used to lie down and spread out her arms and wave them to make angels. You could make beautiful angels in that soft, feathery snow.

Sometimes, after she had gone to bed, she would think about her Secret Place and wonder how it looked in the middle of the night. She thought about it lovingly.

After Afify finished setting the table, Mother told her and Hanna to wash up.

"Your father will be in soon," she reminded. "And you know he likes children clean and neat."

"And polite!" said Afify.

"And polite!"

Father believed in children being very polite. Afify and

Hanna watched their manners after he came home.

They loved him very much for they knew he worked hard to take care of them all.

"God bless our father and save him for us," was a prayer they said every day.

He liked fun, too, when he wasn't tired. Sometimes in the evening he would play his mandolin, his white teeth gleaming. He would call to the children to dance.

Hanna could only stamp and jump. But Afify could really dance; Mother had taught her. She danced gracefully, turning about with her arms in the air, twisting her little hands from her wrists, first up and then down, first left and then right, her bangles chiming. If they were feeling very merry, Mother danced a few steps too, and Father would cry, "Everything should be blackened out!" It was a joke, and meant that Mother was so beautiful he didn't want the Evil Eye to see her. Grandmother would laugh and clap her hands.

"Maybe we will have music tonight," Afify said when Mother was braiding her hair.

"Maybe," Mother answered. She tied fresh ribbons on the ends of the little braids. "But maybe we'll have something else to do."

"What, my Mother?"

"What?" Hanna wanted to know.

Mother wouldn't tell them.

Back in the parlor, Afify went to the window. She pushed aside the starched lace curtains and the heavy red draperies her mother had made. Her mother and grandmother could sew very well. The little flat was full of their handiwork– lace bedspreads, cushions, doilies, and embroidered scarves.

A red tissue-paper wreath, trimmed with silver, was hanging in the window. But this had come from the five-and-ten-cent store.

Afify stood beneath it and looked out with a quiver of awe on the night before Christmas Eve.

November's snow had long since gone. It was misty tonight, almost as though it were raining, and down in the street the headlights of passing cars threw out ribbons of red. Some boys down there were playing Caw Caw Livio.

Afify and Hanna weren't allowed to play in the street, but they knew it very well from the windows.

Opposite was an apartment like their own with fire escapes slanting across it, and a shop on the ground floor. Then came a row of three-story brownstone houses, set wall to wall, with iron railings surrounding the areaways, ash cans in front, and stone stairs leading up to the big front doors.

Afify knew the faces of many of the people who lived there. In the summer women leaned out the windows and called down to the vegetable man, and the banana vendor, and the Italian who pushed a cart full of flowers. Summer and winter, one old man sat all day in a window. A young mother brought a baby to look out. A fat woman in a green dress came to feed a canary.

Tonight there were wreaths or bells in almost all the windows, and Afify saw a Christmas tree in one of them.

"Oh, I hope our father will buy us a Christmas tree!" she thought. Last year, for the first time, he had fallen in with the American custom.

At the nearby corner their street joined Fifth Avenue,

and there was a glow from the strings of colored lights that were hung across that busy thoroughfare. Brooklyn's Fifth Avenue was ablaze with Christmas. Uncle Elias took them to walk there often.

The windows of the shops were crammed with Christmas gifts, and the sidewalks were jammed with people carrying Christmasy bundles, tucked in beside the babies.

Fruits and vegetables were for sale on outdoor stands, and toys, too. The toys were in bins at the edge of the side-walk–dolls in blue, pink, and yellow dresses; baby dolls with blue, pink, and yellow blankets; pandas, elephants, Teddy bears, lambs. Christmas trees were stacked in fragrant rows.

Staring down now, her nose against the pane, Afify saw what seemed to be a walking Christmas tree. It had turned the corner from Fifth Avenue and was approaching their own doorway. She saw, as it came nearer, that a man was carrying it. He turned in at the door.

She ran to her brother and stood before him, dancing. "Hanna! Hanna! Come with me!"

"What is it? Santa Claus?" asked Hanna, scrambling up.

"Something almost as nice. Come! Hurry! You'll see!"

She pulled open the door into the dimly lighted hall.

CHAPTER
2

Grandmother Ends Her Story

Someone was climbing slowly. They could hear the sound of feet, and there was a bumping and swishing, a bumping and swishing.

"I'll bet it *is* Santa Claus," Hanna said hoarsely.

"No. He comes through the window. Besides, I think I know what it is." Afify wiggled the loose tooth.

The bumping and swishing came nearer, and a green feathery mass emerged from the stairway. Beneath it was a glossy black head and the bent figure of a man. He looked up, and they saw their father's eyes, full of pleasure and excitement.

Afify and Hanna shouted with one voice. "Our father's bringing home a Christmas tree!"

"We're going to trim it tonight. That's why I wanted an early dinner." Mother came out, smiling. She took Father's hat that he was carrying, and shooed the children out of the way, and he pulled the feathery mass through the doorway

into the flat.

It threw out cold, and yet it had the fragrance of the Secret Place in summer. Afify ran around it, sniffing, and Hanna jumped until Mother stopped him.

"Be quiet, little donkey! Uncle Abdo will think there is an earthquake."

Hanna ran to Grandmother. "If we have a Christmas tree, Santa will come all right! That old fellow will come! He will come, my Grandmother! I will get a sled."

"Yes, yes!" Grandmother pulled him to her lap and held his plump form close. After a struggle he settled down. It was a good perch to watch from.

Mother ran to spread a sheet in the corner where the tree would stand. She brought out a box with a hole cut in the center that Father had fixed last year to hold the tree. He tried to poke this tree in, but it wouldn't go through, and he sent Afify for the saw.

"It's a bigger tree than last year. Well, you children are bigger, too!" He had patience because it was so close to Christmas Eve.

He sawed and sawed, while Afify wiggled her tooth and Hanna leaned out from Grandmother's lap.

Father put the tree into the box again. This time, it fitted. It was, indeed, bigger than last year's tree. It spiraled triumphantly up to the very ceiling.

Hanna jumped down and he and Afify bounced around it while Father laughed, showing his white teeth, and dusting his hands proudly.

"Now let's eat!" he said at last. "I'll go to wash."

Mother had already returned to the kitchen. She was turning chunks of lamb and onions on a skewer over the gas flame. Afify carried in a bowl of hot green beans, and a bowl of the thick white cheese called leben, and a plate of thin round loaves of Syrian bread. They looked like large pancakes.

Mother helped Grandmother over to the table. "Peace to your hands," Grandmother said.

"And to your hands!" Mother responded.

They took their places behind their chairs, but no one

sat down until Father came.

He strode in presently, his face fresh from soap and water, and his black hair plastered flat. He sat down, and then everyone else sat down.

"Well, well!" he said with a sigh of satisfaction. "We've got a Christmas tree!"

"And the children want to thank you," Mother said.

Thus reminded, they spoke quickly. "Thank you, my Father. We are full of thanks to you."

"You are welcome," said Father, and blessed himself, and the rest did likewise. Then everyone began to eat.

They put the chunks of meat inside the crusty loaves, making a sort of sandwich.

"Our mother finished the pastries," said Afify. "There are five kinds."

"But they're put away," said Hanna. "We haven't had any yet."

"Of course not. The baklava is for Christmas, and it isn't Christmas yet." Father tore off a bit of bread and scooped up some leben and put the whole thing in his mouth.

"I think Santa Claus is going to bring me a sled. Don't you?" asked Hanna.

"Not if you spill so much," said Father, checking Hanna's bold attempt to add beans to his sandwich, which was already very fat.

"Santa's a good guy," grumbled Hanna.

"But he likes little boys to be polite."

"I'm polite. I'm very polite."

Father turned to Afify. "And what do you want for Christmas, my eyes?" That was a pet name he often used.

"Oh, anything!" She twisted her little shoulders, smiling.

"Maybe he will bring you a few pounds," said Father. "Your arms are like matchsticks, and so are your legs." And he tore off another bit of bread and scooped up more leben, and this time he gave it to her.

"I want some leben, too!" cried Hanna.

"You've had some, my foolish."

"But I want my father to fix it for me!"

Father chuckled and gave Hanna some leben in another little spoon of bread. They were all happy, looking now and then at the Christmas tree that stood, tall and gracious, waiting to be trimmed.

They began to trim it as soon as the dishes were done. Afify wiped them while her mother washed.

Uncle Elias came down, but there was no time now for Grandmother to tell how the trees kneel at Christmas. The family was too busy trimming the tree.

First Father put on the lights, winding a green cord

hung with green and red and blue and yellow bulbs in and out among the branches.

When that was finished, the others were allowed to help. They put on balls of every color, fragile as eggshells, and stars and trumpets and birds with spun-glass tails. They put on plastic camels. Grandmother liked those; they reminded her of Lebanon. They sprinkled the branches with silver snow and wound them with golden ropes.

Last of all, Father stood on a chair and fastened the angel to the top.

She was very beautiful, made of paper and tinsel, with long golden hair and big white wings and a pale blue dress that covered her feet.

"Just wait now!" said Father and plugged in the lights.

The room became suddenly magical in a glow of many colors.

They all stood in silence, looking at the shimmering tree. Then Hanna ran to get Bobo to come and see it. But Afify climbed into her grandmother's lap.

She nestled down like a little bird, and Grandmother kissed her fondly. Uncle Elias gave them a mocking smile.

"Now," he asked, "do you want to send her back?"

He often said this to Grandmother when she was petting Afify. He insisted that she had been angry when Afify was born because she wasn't a boy.

"You cried, 'Girl! Girl!' and wept and wailed," Uncle Elias would tease her.

In Lebanon it is very important to have the first child a boy. In fact, boys are generally considered better, and even though Afify was born in Brooklyn, Grandmother had had the Lebanese idea–so Uncle Elias claimed, and Grandmother didn't deny it.

She couldn't exactly deny it because she wouldn't tell a lie. She would just give Uncle Elias a withering look.

She did that now, and cuddled Afify closer. "Any one who would send you back would be mad as a Bedawy!" she murmured.

Afify didn't mind the dispute. She thought it was funny. But now it was wasting time.

"Won't you finish the story, my Grandmother? Wouldn't this be a good time?"

"A very good time," Mother put in. "Just wait until I make some coffee."

She went to the kitchen and returned presently with a long-handled copper pot with four tiny cups on a tray. She poured the coffee–it was Turkish coffee, black and sweet and foamy on the top–and gave some to Father and Uncle Elias and Grandmother and herself.

Hanna got up and snuggled against her. "Maybe," he hinted, "maybe we could have some pastries."

"No, my little one! It isn't Christmas yet."

"Maybe some candy. Maybe a little, little, little piece of halvah." He showed her with his fingers how little it could be.

"No. But you may have some raisins," said Mother, and she brought out a dish filled with raisins and figs. She sat down on the sofa beside Father and smiled at Grandmother.

"Now," she said, "let's have the story!"

Grandmother looked at Uncle Elias, who sat very straight on a straight-backed chair as usual, his right hand on his right knee, his left hand on his left knee, his eyes bright and disrespectful beneath the smoky peak of hair.

"I'll tell the story," she said, "if you'll all keep quiet."

He lifted his palms upward. "Why not? Who wants to make trouble?" He took up his cup.

Hanna took a handful of raisins and sat down under the Christmas tree with Bobo. Afify slipped to the floor and leaned against Grandmother's knee. But she kept darting out to ask questions.

"In Lebanon," Grandmother began, "the trees kneel on every Christmas Eve."

She glanced at Uncle Elias, but Mother was also looking at him. He was silent, and Grandmother continued. "You have to have faith to see it. Not very many have faith enough."

Afify darted out. "What is faith, my Grandmother?"

"Faith is believing. It is knowing that God, Our Creator, can do anything."

"But everyone knows that."

"They ought to, but they don't."

"I have faith," said Afify, pressing her lips firmly.

"So have I," said Hanna, not wanting to be left out.

"God save you for your father and mother!"
Grandmother said, her eyes growing moist. And Father and
Mother murmured tenderly, "God save you!" Even Uncle Elias
seemed pleased.

"Did you see the trees kneel, my Grandmother?"
Afify asked.

"No. I always looked at them when I went out-of-doors
on Christmas Eve to pray. I always hoped to see them kneel,
but I never did. A girl in our village saw them, though. Three
girls saw them, three sisters, but it was because of the faith
of one–"

"Did you know those girls, my Grandmother?"

"Well, I knew them when they were old! And the story
was common knowledge in our village." She glanced at Uncle
Elias again.

"On the Night of the Birth, of course, there are many
wonders. Church bells, we are often told, ring by themselves
on that night. All the waters in the world are holy. And all
the wild beasts become tame. Even a lion or a tiger will not
bite you–"

"I'll bet Bobo would bite you," Hanna interrupted.

"Oh, Hanna! Not on Christmas Eve!"

"No," said Hanna hurriedly. "He wouldn't bite you on Christmas Eve. But any other time he would."

Grandmother did not seem to hear. "On the Night of the Birth," she went on, "angels come down from heaven. The sky is full of them, for those who can see. They come in great armies, holding golden harps, and singing."

"Did you ever see an angel?" Afify darted out again.

"I thought I did sometimes," said Grandmother. "Yes, many things happen on the Night of the Birth.

"The leaven for the year's bread is raised by a miracle that night. In Lebanon, every time a housewife bakes, she saves out a piece of dough to leaven the next batch. But when she bakes before Christmas, she doesn't do this.

"On the Night of the Birth the oldest unmarried daughter is told to get a little flour and mix it with water without yeast. She makes the sign of the cross on it–"

Grandmother made the sign of the cross.

"And she puts it in a clean, fresh handkerchief. Then she hangs it on a tree outside the door. It will come up as though it had yeast. We mix our dough with that all through the year. We save a bit from each baking to use for the next."

Mother nodded. "I remember when my oldest sister did that. I was a little girl in Lebanon."

marie-claude monchaux

Grandmother seemed lost in memory. It was plain that she saw beyond the walls of the room, beyond the walls of Brooklyn, across the ocean, to a flat-roofed village in the foothills of the Lebanons.

"At midnight our mother, God have mercy on her soul, would wake us children. 'Come on now,' she would say, 'we want to pray.' She would take us all out-of-doors to pray. You remember, Elias?" She looked at him with gentle eyes.

"Yes, that I remember," he admitted grudgingly.

"We never closed the door behind us. On Christmas Eve you leave the door open so the Christ Child can come in. We walked up to the hill behind our house.

"Do you remember the stars, Elias? I will never forget the stars in Lebanon. They are like great lamps in the dark blue sky, and they seem so close, so close! It was when look-ing at the stars that I thought I saw angels sometimes–" Grandmother was silent.

Afify flew out once more from the warm nest of Grandmother's skirts. "Was that when you looked to see whether the trees were kneeling?"

"That was when I looked, always. You see, I had heard about these sisters, although they were old when I knew them and it happened when they were young."

"Tell us about it, my Grandmother," said Hanna, who

was hoping that when the story was done Uncle Elias would tell him about Santa Claus.

"There was a little brook, a spring-water brook, on the outskirts of our village," Grandmother continued dreamily. "And one Christmas Eve these sisters went out to bathe."

"Did they go swimming–in the *wintertime*?" Hanna interrupted.

"It wasn't cold in our part of Lebanon in the winter. There was no snow, except on the tops of the mountains. And they wanted to bathe that night because the brook was holy, as all water is on the Night of the Birth. At least, the youngest one wanted to bathe. The two older sisters had no faith."

Grandmother's eyes grew scornful.

"They said to the youngest, 'Oh, you foolish!' But they gave in to her. They went down to the brook and undressed, and the youngest one threw her clothes on a fallen tree. That is, she thought it was a fallen tree. It was a fig tree."

Grandmother, now firm in Mother's support, calmly turned her dark eyes toward Uncle Elias.

He was holding his mouth tightly. When she looked at him he opened it, but he shut it again quickly, like a dog snapping a fly.

Mother jumped up and poured him more coffee.

"And what happened next, my Mother?" she asked.

Grandmother proceeded calmly. "She threw her clothes on this fig tree that she thought was fallen. It was close beside the brook. And they all went into the dark water and bathed and asked for a blessing. And when they came out–!"

Grandmother paused dramatically.

"What had happened, my Grandmother?" asked Afify breathlessly, and Hanna rose up on his knees to listen. He liked this part of the story.

"Her clothes were gone! She looked around, but she couldn't see them anywhere. She couldn't even see the fallen tree. Where that had stood was a tall, straight fig tree. She looked up and there, at the very top, were her garments! The

fig tree hadn't been a fallen tree. It had been kneeling in adoration when she threw her clothes on it. She had been
bathing in the holy water at the very moment the Christ Child
was born."

Grandmother blessed herself, and so did everyone
except Uncle Elias.

"How did she get her clothes down?" demanded Hanna.
"Did she climb the tree? I can climb trees!" He began to
thrash his arms, for he had sat still about as long as he could.

"They got them," Grandmother said. "And when they
had dressed they knelt beside the brook and prayed. The two
older sisters felt ashamed and fearful; their faces were dark.
But the face of the youngest was lighted like an angel's face
when they went home and told the village." She paused.
"The story is repeated there until this day."

Uncle Elias spoke quickly, before Mother had a
chance to stop him.

"The wind could have done it," he said loudly.

"What did you say, my brother?"

"The wind could have blown the clothes upward."

Grandmother looked at him. She looked for a long
time, and when she spoke her voice was sorrowful.

"I don't believe, of course, that it was the wind. But if
it had been the wind, the wind is God's. Who are you and I to

question how He chooses to perform His miracles?

"His miracles are all about us. It is a miracle that we are born. It is a miracle that we see and hear. It is a miracle, my brother, that you continue to live after such blasphemy as you have just now spoken."

"Wah! If you call that–" began Uncle Elias.

"Please!" Mother put in.

Grandmother continued majestically, "The youngest girl had faith. That was why she had asked her sisters to go to the brook in the first place."

"Didn't she even *suspect* that the fig tree was kneeling when she put her clothes on it?" Afify's high little voice was higher than ever in excitement.

"No. She thought it was a fallen tree, and a small one, at that. But when she came out of the water and the tree was upright, she saw that it was tall–for a fig, that is. They are never very big."

"They are ugly, knobby trees. Our Lord cursed them," Uncle Elias muttered.

Mother spoke in a pleading voice. "Uncle Elias, the fig kneels at Christmas like any other tree. God, the Creator, made them all. Figs, and mulberrys, and the buttonwoods that grow on our own Park Slope."

Father got to his feet. Like Hanna he had sat still

long enough.

"And oaks and maples and pines," he said, yawning. "Or any of the trees up in Prospect Park where you take the children."

His voice seemed to Afify to trail away as though he were suddenly speaking from a distance.

She felt choked. Why, if the trees knelt in Brooklyn, the trees in her little Secret Place knelt! They would be kneeling tomorrow night when the world was worshiping the Christ Child at the hour of His birth!

She got up and started to speak, but she stopped. She went into her bedroom.

No light was burning there. It was dark and smelled of attar of roses and the heat in the rumbling radiator. Afify went to her bed, and knelt down.

She blessed herself and looked up where she knew the Virgin Mary hung, fair in her blue and white robes.

Her head felt light, as though it were soaring above her body.

"My father asked me what I wanted for Christmas, and I didn't know. But I know now. I want to see the trees kneel at Christmas. I want to see my own little trees in my little Secret Place kneel. Please, please, Blessed Virgin, let me see them kneel! I have faith–"

But even if she had faith, she thought, how could she see them? She would be here in bed at midnight tomorrow. She might stay awake, but there would be no one to take her to the park. Uncle Elias would be at church with the rest of the grown folks.

An idea so bold that it made her dizzy seemed to come from outside herself. It was as though a voice spoke.

"You could go to the park alone. You know the way."

She did. She knew it well.

Besides, she thought, her heart pounding, the Blessed Virgin would help her.

Suddenly, she was determined to go and see her little trees kneel.

The others were still talking in the parlor. Her own name reached her.

"Afify! Where is the blessed one?"

Afify got up from her knees. She stood very straight, her little shoulders square, her small chin firm.

"I'm going," she announced to Mary, the Virgin, and went out to the parlor.

It was swimming in Christmas-tree light.

"My daughter," Father said, "you forgot to thank your grandmother for the story."

"Thank you, my Grandmother," Afify said.

"What's the matter, my heart?" Mother asked, looking at her closely. "Are you sleepy?"

"I'm not sleepy."

Hanna was at the window.

"Afify! Come here? It's snowing!"

She went to join him. And sure enough, the rain
had turned to snow. A mist of white flakes was whirling in
the darkness. The lights across the street were blurred.

Father came too, and looked out over their heads.

"Snow for Christmas!" he said in a happy voice.

"Snow for Christmas!" said Uncle Elias, rising stiffly.
"Santa had better remember that sled."

"I'm going!" Afify thought, staring out.

The flakes were getting thicker and bigger and fluffier
all the time. They lay on the window ledge as soft as angels'
feathers.

CHAPTER

3

A Trip to the Park

Afify woke early. Grandmother was still asleep, and the room was even darker than usual on a winter morning. This, of course, was because of the snow. It was falling across the window like a heavy curtain. The window ledge was banked with it.

Afify lay quietly in bed, and last night's resolution came rolling over her like an enormous wave.

"I'm going up to Prospect Park tonight. All by myself–or maybe with Hanna. I'm going to see the trees kneel."

She was afraid for a moment. But Afify was almost never afraid. She was very brave in spite of being so small. And she wouldn't let herself be frightened now.

Slipping out of bed, she knelt and blessed herself quickly.

"Please, Blessed Virgin!" she prayed. "Please give me faith enough to see the trees kneel!"

But faith, she thought shivering, wasn't what she need-ed. It was help in getting to the park by herself in the middle of the night.

She knew the trees knelt. People knelt and prayed on Christmas Eve. Cattle did; she had seen them in pictures. Why wouldn't trees be just as religious as people, and cows, and sheep? Of course they knelt!

Maybe, though, she wasn't good enough to see them? Only saints saw them, as a rule, Grandmother seemed to think.

"All right! Then I'll be as good as a saint today," Afify resolved, and she bowed her head again.

"Please, Blessed Virgin, help me to be as good as a saint, and help me to get to the park tonight to see the trees kneel!"

Then she said all the prayers she knew. Usually her morning prayer was only one short one: "God bless our house. God bless our father and keep him for us."

But this morning, after the little prayer, she said an Our Father and a Hail Mary, and the Act of Contrition besides– what she could remember of it.

"There!" she thought, rising. "Those were quite a lot of prayers. I didn't believe saints say any more prayers than that."

She stood straight again, setting her stubborn little jaw.

"Now," she repeated, "I'm going to be as good as a saint!"

She pulled on her underwear and stockings–inside her pink flannel nightgown, to keep warm. She took the nightgown off and hung it up carefully on its special low hook in the closet. She didn't always remember to do that.

She put on last year's warm plaid dress. Mother liked to have her wear it, so she could wear it out, but Afify usually managed to avoid it for it was tight and short.

Putting on her bedroom slippers, so she wouldn't make any noise, she tiptoed to the bathroom. She brushed her teeth–without even being reminded–and looked with interest at the loose one to see if it would be out for Christmas. It would be the sixth tooth she had lost!

She tiptoed to the parlor, and the Christmas tree surprised her. She had forgotten it was there! Even unlighted it cast a magic glow. She walked around it, looking up. "I'm going to see the trees kneel tonight!" she told it in a whisper.

She set the table for breakfast. It wasn't easy to do this in the gray half-light. And she had never set the breakfast table before. In fact, she didn't remember ever having been up ahead of Mother before. She began to feel strange and went and got Hubbooba. "Now what can I do," she thought, "to be especially good?"

She could get out her Learn-To-Count Book and do arithmetic. She had just finished the first column of figures when her mother's door opened.

"Why, Afify! What are you doing up so early, my heart?"

Afify ran over to her. "I set the table," she said, clinging.

"What a good child!"

"I'll wipe the breakfast dishes for you, too. And I've been doing arithmetic. See?"

Mother laughed. "You must think that Santa Claus is looking in the window."

Santa Claus! Afify was annoyed. Little her mother knew what great plan was afoot!

"It's Hanna who likes Santa Claus," she answered stiffly.

Mother ground coffee and set it to boil–they had American coffee in the morning. And pretty soon Father went into the bathroom to shave. Hanna came running out in his pajamas, clutching Bobo.

"Hi! Look at the snow!" he shouted. And he began to march around the parlor, singing. He marched and sang, and marched and sang, making up a song.

Ordinarily Afify would have joined him, marching and singing too, until they both fell down in a heap and had a laughing fit. But Afify was trying to act like a saint, and she doubted that saints had laughing fits.

"Come on, little Hanna, I'll help you dress," she said in such a grown-up tone that he looked at her suspiciously.

"I can dress myself," he said.

"You can't do your shoes."

"I can too!" He threw Bobo at her and ran into his
room and shut the door.

Afify tried hard not to get mad. She pushed at the door
resolutely but Hanna was leaning against it on the other side,
and Hanna was very strong.

"Let me in, little Hanna," she called. But her patient
tone made Hanna more determined than ever to keep her out.
Afify pounded and Hanna pushed, and Afify pushed and
Hanna pounded. And while she was pushing, he sprang away
from the door so that it flew open and he fell down, with Afify
on top of him.

Mother ran out from the kitchen and pulled them both to their feet.

"What a way to start Christmas Eve day!"

Father came out of the bathroom.

"What's going on here?" He sounded cross.

Tears came into Afify's eyes. "I only wanted to help him dress," she said.

"I can dress myself!" Hanna yelled, pulling.

"Hanna!" Mother said, "I think I see Santa Claus looking in."

He stopped struggling. "Where?"

"In the window, of course."

Hanna rolled scared eyes toward the window. "Okeh! You can help me with my shoes," he said to Afify, and she did.

They were standing behind their chairs when Father came to the table.

All morning long Afify and Hanna played under the Christmas tree. It was dark indoors because of the falling snow, so Mother let them plug in the Christmas-tree lights.

They played Santa Claus, because that was the game Hanna liked best since he had stopped playing Indians. Mother gave them a paper sack, and they filled it with old toys, including Bobo and Hubbooba. And Hanna was Santa

Claus and hung it over his shoulder and jumped off a chair
pretending he was coming in the window. Afify just pretended
all the time to be asleep; it wasn't very interesting for her. But
she played it over and over, just the same.

All morning long she never forgot to be as good as a saint.

She kept trying to decide whether to take Hanna along
with her tonight. She didn't need to take him; in fact, he was
pretty young to go. But nothing would happen to him. And it
would be so nice to share the plan with someone!

She couldn't tell him about it yet, though. There was
no chance to talk to him alone.

Grandmother sat in her big chair, crocheting. She was
making a border of lace to edge an altar cloth–first a cross and
then a chalice, then a cross and then a chalice–all the way
around.

Mother was out in the kitchen making kibbee. The
sound of her pounding rang through the little flat. She was
pounding onions that later would be added to lean ground
lamb, spices, white pine nuts from Lebanon, and crushed
wheat, which was now soaking in water.

It wouldn't be baked until tomorrow. It was for
Christmas dinner.

"Are we having turkey, too?" Afify asked, for most
of the girls at school had turkey for Christmas.

"Yes, we're having turkey. But I'm going to stuff it in the Lebanese way with rice and meat," Mother replied.

Hanna cried that he wanted to see the pastries. And Mother opened the cupboard door and gave them both a peek. One kind was shaped like a pie, layer on thin crusty layer, with crushed nuts between, drenched in honey. One kind had pistachio centers. Others were round with holes in the center like doughnuts. Eat and Be Grateful, which Hanna liked best, had almonds inside. Afify liked best the one called Nest of a Bird.

Hanna teased for a taste, but Afify didn't. She was acting like a saint. And anyway Mother refused.

"Not until tonight," she said, putting them away. "You can have some tonight with the company, before we tuck you into bed and go to Mass."

She smiled at them when she said that–so sweetly that Afify felt a queer guilty pang. Yet she knew there was no reason to feel guilty. It was a holy thing to do, to go out and see the trees kneel.

But it was strange, just the same, to have a secret from Mother. She longed more and more to share it with Hanna.

Outside it was still snowing, harder than ever. The roofs across the way were covered, and so were the parked cars below, and the street, and the sidewalk. Men were shoveling down there.

It certainly didn't look like a going-out day. But Afify was anxious to go. She not only wanted a chance to talk to Hanna; she wanted to see just exactly how long it took them to get to the park. She had never noticed, and tonight she would need to know.

She mentioned a walk but Mother was emphatic in refusing. "Of course not! This is a day for staying snug at home."

Afify couldn't tease for she was acting like a saint. Fortunately, though, Hanna teased.

"Please, my Mother, I want to go out. I'll put on my cowboy boots."

"I'll put on my boots, too," Afify promised.

"No!" Mother said. "I'm sorry, but you can't possibly go."

That sounded final. Afify began to worry. She went into her bedroom, shut the door, and looked at the blue and white figure above her bed.

"Please, Blessed Virgin, I just have to go out! It's on account of–you know what–tonight!"

Blessing herself, she went back to Hanna, and as they played and ate their lunch, she kept glancing toward the window.

While they were eating, the sun came out. It threw

a sudden, cheerful shaft of light all the way across the parlor. Both children ran to the window.

It had stopped snowing! The sky was still mistily gray around the edges but higher up the clouds were pearly white. And at the very top the sky was triumphantly blue.

"It's cleared up!" they shouted. "Mother! Come and see!"

She looked out and saw the patch of blue, and the sunshine making the new snow sparkle.

"All right." She gave in. "If you can talk Uncle Elias into taking you."

With whoops of joy Hanna and Afify ran upstairs and pounded at the door of Uncle Charles's flat. Aunt Esther answered, and said that Uncle Elias wasn't there. He was down at Uncle Abdo's.

The children raced down two flights and found the old men smoking a narghile.

It stood on the floor between them, a big glass bottle filled with water. On top of it, in a copper bowl, a live coal rested like an egg on a nest of tobacco. It was a damp nest. They had often seen Aunt Shafeah, preparing a pipe for herself or Uncle Abdo, wash the Turkish tobacco before she stuffed it in. They liked to watch her do it and see her heat the charcoal over the gas flame.

A snakelike tube, tufted with green and yellow, led

up to the smoker's mouth. Uncle Abdo and Uncle Elias exchanged it sociably. It wasn't necessary to smoke together in this way. There were several of the big pipes in the room. But it was pleasant sharing a pipe with a relative or friend, passing the tube back and forth in cozy intimacy.

The smoke, drawing through the water, made a bubbling sound, and the tobacco smelled good, too. The children liked the narghile, but Uncle Elias got up quickly when they came in. He acted embarrassed.

"I just thought I'd keep the old fellow company," he said in English. Uncle Abdo didn't speak any English.

He took his pipe out of his mouth.

"How is your honored grandmother?" he asked in Arabic.

"She's very well, my Uncle, thanks be to God!" Afify replied.

Hanna had already pounced on Uncle Elias. "We want to go out! We want to go out!"

"And Mother says we may if you will take us," Afify explained. She added, making her voice very sweet, "It's turned into a *beautiful* day!"

"A beautiful day!" Uncle Elias exclaimed. "What do you mean? It's a snowstorm!"

"No, no! It's cleared up!" Afify insisted, and they pulled him toward the window. He looked up at the patch of blue. It

was very small, not much larger than a handkerchief, but it
was very bright.

"Okeh, okeh!" he grumbled, and the children ran for the
door, but Afify remembered to act like a saint. She ran back
and said good-by politely to Uncle Abdo.

"I hope you won't be lonely," she added.

"No, my little one." Uncle Abdo picked up his newspaper. It was printed in Arabic and he read it from right to left
instead of from left to right as Afify read her schoolbooks.
"I will be content with my narghile and my newspaper. Go,
in the keeping of God!"

The children pounded up the stairs. Afify's little
matchlike legs raced Hanna's chubby ones. They put on their
snow suits, and mittens, and wound scarves around their necks.

"Remember to put the earflaps down," Mother said
when Hanna put on his cap.

With panting and groaning they pulled on their boots.
Hanna's were red, but cut exactly like Hopalong Cassidy's.
That was why he called them his cowboy boots.

"Come here!" Mother said to Afify. "I'll tuck your skirts
into your snow pants." They always seemed to hang outside
unless Mother tucked them in.

At last they were ready. Mother kissed them both.
She gazed into Afify's little face, which looked smaller than

ever with a scarf tied tightly around it.

"Are you sure you feel well?"

"Oh yes!" Afify answered. She tried to make her smile very wide and bright; and fortunately Uncle Elias came down just then wearing his heavy coat and overshoes.

"You're good to take them out!" said Mother.

"Good! I'm crazy!" Uncle Elias answered. But he put his hat, as usual, on the side of his head. And once outside he began to whistle "Rudolph, the Red-Nosed Reindeer."

It was very nice outside. There was snow over everything. Plenty had come to take the place of all that had been shoveled away. It was soft as down, twinkling in the sunshine. Hanna stamped through it, making tracks in his cowboy boots. But Afify stayed close to Uncle Elias.

"How long does it take us to get to the park?"

"Oh, about twenty minutes!"

Twenty minutes! Then they ought to leave home tonight at twenty minutes to twelve. But how would she know when it was twenty minutes to twelve?

"My Uncle!" she said. "Would it take me very long to learn to tell time?"

"No. I'll teach you some day." He winked at her. "The most important thing is having a watch."

At Sixth Avenue Hanna waited for them. He and Afify

weren't allowed to cross the street without Uncle Elias. At Seventh Avenue they waited again–Seventh Avenue had a trolley–and again at Eighth Avenue, for that had buses. It was a one-way street and the buses and automobiles all went very fast.

Afify watched carefully everything Uncle Elias did. She kept remembering that tonight she must know just how to go. For she would be taking care of Hanna! She must take good care of Hanna. He was pretty little to go to the park at midnight.

Between Eighth Avenue and Prospect Park West, the houses were very attractive. The shining windows showed beautiful wreaths and glimpses of Christmas trees. There were buttonwood trees planted in a row along the street. They were curious trees, with trunks that were always peeling, and little balls clinging to their branches even in the winter. Today, though, the balls were hidden by the snow that lay in white layers on the branches.

Prospect Park West had big stone mansions, looking across at the park. This was the crossing that worried Afify most. The wide avenue was crowded with traffic. It was another one-way street, and the cars went like the wind.

"There ought to be a stop sign here," Uncle Elias always said. "It's a very dangerous crossing."

He said it today, looking worried, for the street was

slushy and cars were sluing about.

"I must remember," Afify thought.

After a long wait he got them safely to the other side.

They scrambled, as they always did, to the wall enclosing the park and walked along on top of it, knocking off the snow. Everything that had been able to catch snow was holding it. It weighed down the trees and the bushes.

At the gate, which had tall posts with statues of wild animals on top, they jumped down into the park. Hanna wanted to go at once to the coasting, but Afify whispered to him.

"Come on up to the C.P. first. I have a secret to tell you."

"Huh?" asked Hanna.

"A secret! It's important. Come along!"

Uncle Elias seemed glad to sink down on his bench, although there wasn't a single mother out today, and Afify and Hanna wallowed through the drifts.

The trees in the little Secret Place cast soft blue shadows. And like all the other trees, they held soft cushions of snow. Snow was wedged into every tiny crevice of their branches. It was beginning to melt, though. The day was growing warm.

"What's the secret?" Hanna asked.

She looked mysterious. "Have you noticed, Hanna, that I've been awfully good all day?"

He nodded doubtfully.

"Well! I've been trying to act like a saint."

"What do you want to do that for?" asked Hanna. "I don't think saints are much fun."

"I think the trees kneel at Christmas here, too. I think they kneel in Brooklyn just the same as they do in Lebanon."

He was interested now. "No kidding! I wish I could see them."

"Which one would you rather see?"

"Why, the biggest one in the park!"

"I wouldn't," said Afify. "I'd rather see these little trees right here in our Secret Place. And I'm coming up to see them!"

"Huh?"

"I'm coming up tonight, at midnight. You can come too, if you want to."

He looked puzzled. "But Uncle Elias will be in church," he said.

"I know. We would have to come by ourselves."

He stared at her.

"Don't think," said Afify quickly, "that it wouldn't be all right to do. Of course, nobody must know until we've done it. It will have to be a secret until then. But after we get home and tell how the trees kneeled, nobody's going to be mad. Do you think the mother of those three girls who saw the trees kneel in Lebanon was mad when they got home?"

"And we wouldn't even go swimming," said Hanna. Plainly he accepted the plan.

"No. It's too cold. And there's no brook anyway. We'll just come up here and see our little trees kneeling."

"Probably," said Hanna, "we'll see Santa Claus, too. He'll be galumping across the sky with those reindeer."

"Well," said Afify, "you must remember that we're not *looking* for Santa Claus. If we happen to see him, of course, it's all right. But we're out to see the trees kneel."

She grew serious. "And that reminds me of what I was going to say about being a saint. Our grandmother thinks that only saints see the trees kneeling. That's why I've been trying to be as good as a saint. Will you try, too?"

"Okeh!"

"I think, maybe, we'd better pray now."

"Okeh!" said Hanna.

So they got down on their knees in the snow. It was very deep and made the knees of their snow suits wet.

When they got up Afify found a stick and printed in the snow, "Tonite!"

"That's so our little trees will know we're coming," she said.

Uncle Elias called just then. "Hi, kids! Where are you?"

He started up the slope. But Afify and Hanna ran down quickly.

"Don't let him catch on!" Afify whispered. "Remember, we mustn't tell a soul!"

The sun was gone by the time they got out of the park. The whole sky was gray again, but the snow was still melting.

It dripped from the buttonwoods and made little puddles in the drifts. The streets were slushier than ever.

Christmas trees had been lighted in some of the windows.

"It begins to seem like Christmas Eve," Uncle Elias said. And when they reached their own door he went past it, and took them around the corner to Fifth Avenue, and bought them candy canes.

Fifth Avenue with its strings of colored lights, the happy hurrying people, the crowded fruit and candy stores and the almost empty bins of toys seemed thrillingly like Christmas Eve. It made Afify feel as though she had a little bird inside her. Telling Hanna about the plan had made it seem very real. But having Christmas Eve suddenly happen this way brought it fearsomely close.

It was getting misty, almost rainy, now and Uncle Elias took them home. Mother was standing in front of the chest in the parlor.

"I'm making the shrine," she called.

She made it every year.

She cleared the top of the chest and hung a crucifix above it. Then she put photographs of Afify and Hanna on either side and holy candles in front. She would not light them until Father came in.

She knelt down beside the children, helping them off with their mittens and snow suits and boots.

"How wet you are! You must go and change your shoes and stockings right away."

But she did not let them go. Instead, she put her arms around them and hugged them tight, kissing their soft, cold cheeks.

"God save you for your father and mother! Happy

Christ's Birthday!" she said.

"Happy Christ's Birthday!" they shouted.

CHAPTER

4

Christmas Eve Indoors

*I*t is easier to do something hard than it is to wait for the time to begin it, Afify thought, setting the table. It seemed as though she could not wait until the grownups started for mid-night Mass! And so much had to happen first! Dinner, and the dishes, and dressing up, and company. There was always company, coming and going, on Christmas Eve.

All the Haddad relatives came–that was Mother's family–because Grandmother lived with them, and she was old and important. And all the Shehadi uncles and aunts came. They were Father's brothers and sisters. Cousins from both sides, of all ages, came too. And there would be refreshments tonight–for those who were not fasting.

Fasting! Afify almost dropped the plate of bread she was placing on the table. She must remember to fast! A saint would certainly fast on a night she hoped to see the trees kneel.

She would have to eat a little something, of course, or Mother would get worried. But she would eat as little as she could.

It wouldn't be hard. She wasn't hungry. That little bird inside of her, fluttering harder and harder, took away her appetite. This was lucky, for they were having yabra for dinner, and it was very good.

Grapevine leaves were stuffed with rice and meat and white pine nuts. They were rolled like cigarettes and arranged neatly in the pot, on top of a pile of bones (to give flavor). They simmered in a little water, throwing off a tempting smell. It drifted through the dining room now, but Afify wasn't tempted.

At supper she ate only a few bites.

Mother noticed it. "What's the matter, my heart?"

"Oh, I'm just not hungry!" Afify shrugged, as though it were of no importance.

"I'll fix her some bread and leben," said Father, and he did. And, of course, she had to eat that. But then she stopped eating again.

Hanna shouted that he wanted Father to fix *him* some leben, and Father laughed, but Mother still looked at Afify with anxious eyes.

"You don't seem like yourself today," she said, and Afify felt her cheeks grow hot. She thought again how strange it was to have a secret from Mother. She didn't like it, but it couldn't be helped.

There was another frightening moment when Father remarked that it was turning cold. If the streets froze, after the rain and all that melting, it would be bad, he said. Perhaps Grandmother ought not to go to church.

Afify could scarcely breathe until Grandmother answered. What would she do, she thought in panic, if Grandmother stayed at home? How could she manage to get to the park if Grandmother were sleeping in her big bed beside Afify's little one?

It turned out all right. Grandmother said without hesitation that she was going.

"Our Blessed Lord will take care of me. You know, my son-in-law, I am eighty-two years old. There will not be many more Christmases when I can worship at the Birth."

"God save you," said Mother, blessing herself.

"God save you," murmured Father.

"And I may as well say now," Grandmother continued, "that I want to start early. I want to sit in my usual seat and not find it taken by one of those Christians who go to church only on Christmas and Easter!" She looked scornful.

"We'll start early," Mother assured her. And Afify was glad to hear that. She would be put to bed before the family left for church. And she couldn't get up to dress for the park until everyone was gone. Getting up and dressing and helping Hanna to dress would take time.

"Yes," she chimed in eagerly. "I think you ought to start *very* early. I think our grandmother ought to have her very own seat."

"Oh, you do, do you?" Father asked, smiling.

They hurried with the dishes, for they had to dress up for the evening. Father put on his best blue suit and a striped blue and yellow tie. With his black hair oiled and his shoes polished to a shine he looked very handsome.

Mother helped Grandmother into her best black silk, trimmed with jet beads. She combed Grandmother's fleecy hair; and Grandmother put on her diamond earrings and her bracelets, and sprinkled herself with attar of roses. Mother helped her out to her big chair in the parlor, and she sat there with her cane by her side, to wait.

Hanna wore his best suit too, and a new plaid tie and knitted socks that left his fat knees bare. His shoes shone like Father's, for Father had polished them also. Mother brushed Hanna's hair until it gleamed above his scrubbed, rosy face. She took him out to Grandmother.

"Please try to keep him clean until the company comes," she said.

Grandmother patted him gently. "He will be a good boy tonight because the Christ Child is being born of the Virgin Mary in a cave."

"Oh, I'm going to act like a saint!" Hanna exclaimed, and Father laughed out loud. Mother and Grandmother looked amazed, and Afify's heart almost turned over. She shook her head wildly.

"He's thinking about Santa and that sled," chuckled Father.

Hanna squirmed. He remembered now that he shouldn't have said it. He did act almost like a saint, though. He didn't rush about or roll on the floor. He sat still and kept himself clean.

Mother wanted Afify to wear her new red wool, but Afify wanted to wear her sweater and skirt. She thought they made her look bigger and older.

"Please let me wear my sweater and skirt for Christmas Eve!" she pleaded, and as usual she got her own way.

She stood very straight, reminding herself as she did in school sometimes, "I'm seven years old even if I'm *not* seven years big."

She put on her best bracelet of lacy silver filagree. This was valuable; it came from Lebanon, it wasn't like the bangles she wore every day. It stretched in such a way that she would be able to wear it even when she grew up.

"Now don't wiggle that loose tooth!" Mother said, sending her to the parlor. "We don't want it to come out and leave a big hole for Christmas."

And Afify went out and sat quietly in front of the Christmas tree.

Mother dressed herself in her best purple silk and put on her diamond earrings. They weren't as large as Grandmother's, but they were diamonds; Father was very proud of them. She put on bracelets too, and rubbed black around her eyes as Lebanese women do. It made them look even larger and blacker than they were.

Only her hair with its heavy wreath of braids looked like the every-day Mother.

As soon as she was dressed she began to arrange pastries on two of her best gold-edged plates.

"I'll help you, my Mother," Hanna called when he saw what she was doing.

"You may come and watch," she said, and gave him a crumb of baklava.

Before she had finished, the doorbell started ringing, and the relatives began to arrive.

"Happy Christ's Birthday!" some of them said in Arabic.

"Merry Christmas!" others cried in English.

Father greeted them with beautiful phrases. "I am honored to have you in my house," he said to one, and to the next: "Come in! This is your home! I'll go outside."

Of course, it wasn't their home and he didn't intend to go out, but that was nice to say.

The relatives replied with phrases equally gracious, such as "Peace to your house!" or "God save your children and your family!"

Each new arrival kissed Grandmother. "Peace to your age," they said; or sometimes, "May God give you many more holidays."

The uncles, aunts, and cousins weren't always so polite. In fact, they were never together long without an argument. But this was the Night of the Birth. In a solemn sort of way,

it was a party.

Not the kind of a party, of course, that they had on New Year's Eve. Then nobody fasted, and Father played the mandolin and Uncle Salom the drum, or they put Lebanese records on the phonograph, and everyone sang and danced.

Tonight was quieter. Some of the women carried prayer books. The candles flickered in front of the children's pictures in the shrine. And everyone was aware that the Christ Child would be born soon.

Packages piled up beneath the Christmas tree, and soon the small parlor rang with the relatives' voices. How the *r*'s trilled, and how hands flashed, for Lebanese talk partly with their hands, showing you how big or how small, how high or how low everything is!

The relatives made Afify think of a flock of birds, some-times. They were so noisy and lively and bright.

Uncle Elias wore a red tie. He was erect and jaunty in a well-pressed suit.

"He's going to flirt with the girls in the choir," Uncle Charles joked.

Uncle Charles, trim and clean shaven, looked just like an American. So did Aunt Esther, thin and smart, an orchid pinned to her black dress. But Uncle Abdo, with his leathery face, and little old Aunt Shefeah, with her head wrapped in a scarf, looked even more Lebanese than usual.

Uncle Yusef was large and dignified. He walked up and down with his hands beneath his coat in back, showing a silver watch chain. Uncle Askander had a straight black mustache laid like a pencil across his upper lip. Uncle Salom had a thin, melancholy face. (But it gleamed when he played the drum on New Year's Eve. He played it with his hands.)

The uncles were very different from each other, but almost all the aunts were plump. Most of them were pretty, too, with large dark eyes, earrings, and jingling bracelets.

Even prettier were the teen-age girl cousins. Afify watched them admiringly, and so did Uncle Elias. They had curly black hair, liquid eyes, dimples, and snowy teeth. Their bright-colored dresses were in the latest style.

One boy cousin, Michiel, had a brand-new small mustache.

"Mike must have a girl!" the others teased.

"Sure I have, and here she is!" He leaned down to hook his arm in Afify's. She was glad he didn't pick her up and swing her, as relatives usually did. She walked around with him, beaming with pride, and forgot for a while to act like a saint.

Mother passed thin, tiny cups of the foamy Turkish coffee. Some of the men took wine in little glasses. She set out black olives, and pistachio nuts both plain and sugared, and chickpeas rolled in sugar, and–at last–the pastries!

Hanna and Shebil, the cousin near his age, shrieked with joy at the pastries. Shebil grabbed a Bird's Nest and Hanna, an Eat and Be Grateful.

Shebil's mother shook him, but gently, because it was

Christmas Eve. "Now, none of that, or the camel will get you!" she said.

Mother was too busy to notice. She was bringing in cakes of glazed nuts, and jellylike candies, dusted with sugar, and halvah. She urged everyone to eat.

"Won't you have just a little? It's not near time for Mass."

Some of the people weren't going to church, and they ate freely. Uncle Elias *was* going to church, but he ate freely anyway, under Grandmother's disapproving eye. Some of the others who were going to church nibbled just a little. (They weren't receiving communion, of course.) But some of the uncles, aunts, and cousins would touch nothing at all.

It depended, Afify knew, upon what rite you observed–Syriac or Maronite or Melchite or Latin or Orthodox. Some rites were stricter than others. It was strange to have so many kinds of religion in one family, but in Lebanon, when a woman married, she took her husband's rite.

"And what does it matter," Grandmother often said, "so long as we love God–and our neighbor."

Grandmother and Mother were fasting, Afify observed. And when the plates were passed to her, she shook her head resolutely.

"What's the matter, my little love? You're not going to church."

"I know," Afify answered.

"Are you sure you feel well?"

"Oh yes! I feel fine." But she was really beginning to feel queer. For a while she had forgotten, in the excitement of the party, about the plan for going to the park. But it wouldn't be long now–

"My Grandmother," she asked, "isn't it almost time you started for Mass?"

But even Grandmother thought it was too early. Everyone was having such a good time.

The children were beside themselves with joy because of the sweets. Treats such as these weren't offered to them often. Only on a holiday or for a wedding or like celebration were cupboard doors unlocked.

Hanna and Shebil were competing.

"I ate the most!"

"No, I did!"

"No, me! Me!"

They pretended to shoot each other and fell dead.

The fat baby sucked on a black olive.

While they ate, the men talked business.

"God is giving bounteously," Uncle Yusef said, meaning that things were going well.

He manufactured negligees and Uncle Askander sold them. Uncle Charles was in the confectionery business. Uncle Salom and Father had a laces-and-white-goods store, and Uncle Abdo imported pistachio nuts.

In the old days several of them had gone through the country, peddling. They liked to tell stories about those adventurous times. None of them did it any more except

Cousin Mike, who was peddling laces to put himself through college.

While the men talked business, the women in a little circle talked of holy things. They told of vows that had made sick people well. Grandmother, when Mother was sick one time, had vowed to sleep in the church. That was common in Lebanon, but the American priest wouldn't let her do it.

"We don't do it in Brooklyn," he had explained.

Mother had recovered anyway.

One aunt had promised a saint a candle as high as her husband if her husband should get well of an ailment he had. He had recovered too, and she had given the candle, although he was a tall man—over six feet high.

Grandmother told again about the oldest daughter in the household making the dough on Christmas Eve. Afify leaned toward her and whispered, "I'm the oldest daughter, my Grandmother."

But Grandmother shook her head sadly. "There's no use making dough in Brooklyn. We don't bake bread at home."

It was true. The round flat loaves came from the Lebanese bakery.

The holy stories made Afify think with little shivers of her own vow.

"My Grandmother," she said again, "isn't it almost time

to start for Mass?"

This time Grandmother answered, "Wah! Maybe it is!" and looked around at the clock.

Mother spoke quickly. "You know, my Mother, last year we went so early that we almost fell asleep before the Mass began."

"I didn't fall asleep. I was saying my prayers," Grandmother replied. "And I don't want to lose my seat to one of those Christians who come only on Christmas and Easter."

But before the matter was decided, the sound of music floated into the room. It was one of the Christmas carols Afify had learned in school:

"It came upon the midnight clear,

That glorious song of old—"

Father went to the window and threw it up.

Down in the snowy street a group of people were singing. Their voices rose pure and sweet.

"They come every year," Father said softly. "It's a church group."

The carolers went from one song to another.

The older people had not known these songs in Lebanon. But they had come to love them during the years in the New World. Everyone listened reverently.

Father had taken Hanna on his lap. Mother leaned against Grandmother's chair.

> *"Silent night, Holy night!*
> *All is calm, all is bright,*
> *'Round yon Virgin Mother and Child—"*

Afify's heart swelled.

She saw the manger and the swaddled Christ Child. She saw the heavens full of angels, and the shepherds and the cattle kneeling. She was very, very glad she had decided to go to see the trees kneel.

The music stopped and Father closed the window.

"They were good to come out tonight," he said. "The streets are wicked. All that melting this afternoon, and now it has frozen."

"Yes," replied Aunt Esther. "They're talking about an ice storm on the radio."

Uncle Yusef went to the window. He turned around, shaking his head. "I don't think Mother ought to go out," he declared. He was Grandmother's son.

"That's what I told her at dinner," Father said.

Uncle Yusef went over to Grandmother, and Afify shut her eyes.

"She has to go! She has to go, dear Blessed Virgin!" she prayed.

Uncle Yusef was so important! He had such a commanding way of speaking! He could persuade Grandmother if anyone could.

But Grandmother's lips tightened, as Afify's did sometimes. Perhaps she was like Afify, or Afify was like her, about being determined.

"I'll go, in the keeping of God!" she announced, lifting her cane.

So that was settled! And at last the company began to leave. They went to the bedrooms and took their wraps from the lace spreads and said they would see each other tomorrow, if they lived. They wished each other "Merry Christmas" and "Happy Christ's Birthday," but still they stood, talking.

Afify and Hanna said good night to everyone, and Mother helped Hanna into his flannel pajamas. He jumped into bed, but as soon as she left him he jumped out and ran back to the parlor. He knew he wouldn't be scolded on Christmas Eve. And he rushed about, and took another pastry, and ran to the window to look for Santa Claus.

"Doesn't he remember?" Afify thought despairingly. "Doesn't he know it takes *time* to get to the park? We'll never get there by midnight if he doesn't settle down!"

She took off her sweater and skirt, but she left on her underwear and stockings. She put her nightgown on right

over them and said her prayers quickly. That wasn't a good
way to say them on such an important night but she was afraid
Grandmother would see her underwear.

Grandmother was pinning on her hat, and in a moment
Mother came in from putting Hanna to bed a second time.
She helped Grandmother into her coat and bent to kiss Afify.

"Hanna is asleep already!" she said. "It's almost eleven
o'clock–pretty late for a little boy five years old."

"How much before eleven is it, my Mother?"

"Oh, ten minutes or so!"

"But I mean, exactly."

"Why do you want to know exactly?" Mother laughed
and stood aside so Grandmother could kiss her.

Father came in to kiss her, too. Afify clung to him with
her little soft arms. He was so big and strong! She wished he
were going with them to the park.

"Happy Christ's Birthday!" Father said softly. "Get to
sleep now, my eyes. Uncle Charles will be upstairs if you
need him."

"Isn't he going to church?" Afify demanded. She sat
upright, and Father might have seen her underwear peeping
out above her nightgown. But he didn't notice it, and she lay
down again quickly.

"Oh, he isn't going to Mass until tomorrow," Father said.

This was a shock. It made things harder, to have to get outdoors without waking Uncle Charles.

Afify pulled up the covers, and listened to the company departing. Soon they were all gone, except for the group that was going to church with Grandmother. The lights were turned out except for the one left burning in the parlor. The door to the hall opened–she heard a radio downstairs playing Christmas music. And it closed again. She heard the click of the night catch.

"They forgot," she thought, "to leave the door open for the Christ Child."

She heard their steps and voices growing fainter. Then it was silent in the Shehadi flat.

"Now–now," she thought, "we must get up and go to the park!"

marie-claude

CHAPTER

5

Christmas Eve Outdoors

*I*t was hard to wake Hanna. He was sleeping soundly after the exciting evening. He was sprawled across the bed on his stomach, Bobo pinned down by one arm, his head turned so that a pink cheek and softly breathing mouth were visible.

Afify stood beside him, shivering. She shook his flannel shoulder.

"Hanna! Wake up! We're going to the park."

Hanna murmured something without opening his eyes.

Afify continued to shake him. At last he sat up, blinking.

"Hurry, Hanna! We haven't got much time."

"Okeh," said Hanna hoarsely.

He stared at her, and slowly, she could see, he began to remember the plan. He jumped out of bed and took off his pajamas and began to pull on his underwear. He worked like a boy in a dream, but at least he was dressing fast.

Afify ran back to her room and shucked off her night-gown. She was glad she had left her underwear on. There was nothing to put back on but the sweater and skirt and her shoes. Her braids were mussy, but the ribbons still held.

She met Hanna in the shadowy parlor. Without speaking, they went to the closet for their wraps. They sat down on the floor and pulled on snow pants. Hanna put on his cowboy boots. He struggled into his coat and jammed his cap on his head.

"Pull down the earflaps," Afify reminded him, as their mother always did. "And wear your scarf."

"Okeh," said Hanna. He wound it around his neck and got out his mittens.

"I want to take Bobo," he said suddenly.

"All right," Afify answered.

She had her snow suit on now, but there was no mother to tuck in her little skirts. They hung outside the pants. She buttoned her coat and tied a scarf on her head, pulled on her boots and felt for her own mittens.

She wished she knew what time it was. Maybe, she thought, she ought to take a watch. She knew where Mother kept her watch, in a drawer in her bureau.

She found it and shook it as Mother always did and put it into her pocket, since it was too big for her wrist.

"I thought we ought to have a watch," she said to Hanna, who nodded.

Some of the sleep was leaving him now. He looked up at the unlighted tree, and underneath it where the relatives' presents were piled.

"No sled yet," he said.

"Oh, Santa Claus hasn't come!" said Afify. "I haven't even been to sleep."

"Maybe we'll see him!" said Hanna, brightening. "Maybe we'll see those reindeer galumping through the sky."

"Maybe," said Afify. "Be very quiet now! Uncle Charles is at home and we don't want him to hear us." She opened the door.

"It's got the lock on," Hanna said huskily. "Just shut it! It will lock."

"I don't think we'd better shut it. You remember what Grandmother says. In Lebanon they leave it open in case the Christ Child wants to come in."

"Christ Child! Santa Claus! Heck, what a lot of people are coming!" Hanna replied in a whisper.

They stole down softly.

The stairs were very dark. The only light came from the entrance hall, two flights below. There was no sound from Uncle Charles's flat above, and Uncle Abdo's, of course, was empty. Someone was at home at the Giovannis', though. The radio was going.

They reached the downstairs hall and opened the door.

It was strange to be outside all alone in the dark and the cold. The buildings across the way were spangled with lighted windows. There were Christmas trees showing, too.

The snow in the gutters glittered strangely. It seemed to be covered with a thin, sugary glaze. The sidewalk was a glare of ice and so was the street.

"Everything seems to be varnished."

Hanna whispered, although there was no need to whisper any more. He hugged Bobo tight.

The street was empty. There wasn't a car or a person in sight. Afify took his hand and they started to walk toward the park. They walked as fast as they could but it was hard to make progress; the walk was so slippery.

"I'm glad we put on our boots," Afify said.

But even with boots, if you took two steps you slipped back one.

Hanna was looking up, higher than the lighted windows, higher than the roofs, all the way to the sky where distant stars were shining.

"Do you see Santa Claus, Afify?"

"No, I don't see him. And we must watch where we're going," Afify said. For they had reached Sixth Avenue, where there was usually traffic. But there didn't seem to be much traffic tonight. The avenue was almost empty. Like their own street, it was a sheet of ice. Afify and Hanna slipped and slid across it.

"Besides," said Afify as they went on toward Seventh, "maybe we shouldn't be thinking about Santa Claus just now. You know, Hanna, there are angels in the sky on Christmas Eve."

"No kidding!" said Hanna, although he knew it perfectly well. Grandmother had told them so often.

"We couldn't miss them," he went on, looking up. "They've got big white wings."

"And golden hair," said Afify.

"And rings around their heads."

"And they wear long dresses that cover their feet."

"I know one angel's name. It's Gabriel. I'd just as soon see Gabriel if I can't see Santa Claus," Hanna said generously.

The traffic light at Seventh Avenue was red. It poured a lavish stream of red along the frozen street. Afify and Hanna waited while the trolley rattled past, the light from its windows splintering into fragments on the ice.

When the traffic light turned green, they started across. "Look!" cried Hanna. "We can skate on these streets."

"We can skate without skates!" Afify added in an ecstatic treble.

They ran and slid, and ran and slid again, until they reached the other side.

No one paid any attention to them. In fact there weren't many people out. Hanna mentioned this when they were walking on again.

"Well," said Afify, "the children are all asleep, and the grown folks are in church, I suppose. There are lots of churches in Brooklyn. It's the City of Churches. I heard that in school."

"There's a man who isn't in church," Hanna replied.

He had turned the corner from Eighth Avenue and was walking toward them. He was slipping and sliding even more than they were.

"Hi! Merry Chris'mas!" he called in a funny whistling voice.

"Merry Christmas!" Afify and Hanna answered politely.

He stopped, but he couldn't stand up straight.

"You kids–know where you're going?"

"Yes, sir," Afify answered.

"Where?"

She didn't want to say that they were going to the park.

"We have an appointment," she replied with dignity. They certainly did! A wonderful appointment!

The man laughed and laughed.

"Oh, they have an appointment!" he said, as though he were speaking to someone else. "Tha's good! They have an appointment. Well, goo'-by, kids! Merry Chris'mas!"

"Merry Christmas!" said Afify and Hanna, and he zigzagged down the street.

They came to Eighth Avenue and looked both ways. There wasn't a bus in sight. A few cars passed, their head-lights hurling glimmery spears along the ice. Someone waved from one of the cars but at last the coast was clear.

"We can skate some more!" cried Hanna, and they skimmed across the street. Hanna let Bobo run and slide. "Bobo thinks it's fun," he said.

That reminded Afify of something.

"If we should see any lions or tigers in the park, don't worry, Hanna. All the animals are tame tonight, you know."

"I know," he answered. "Bobo isn't even growling." He looked back longingly across the gleaming street. "Bobo would like to skate some more."

"There isn't time," Afify answered. She stopped under the street lamp and looked at Mother's watch.

"What time is it?" asked Hanna.

Afify shook the watch and held it to her ear. "I don't exactly know but I think it's almost midnight. We'd better go on."

They had come to the block with the buttonwood trees. Hanna looked around him.

"These trees aren't kneeling," he remarked.

"No. It isn't midnight yet. They're getting ready, though. They're looking awfully pretty."

"Yes, they are."

They had the shiny varnished look that everything had tonight. The snow on their branches had that sugary glaze. And where the snow was gone the twigs looked glassy. Even the little balls seemed to have turned to glass.

The long row of buttonwood trees glimmered in the lights from the windows. Some glimmered red and green and blue, for some of the houses were trimmed with colored lights.

They made Afify think of the beauty that lay ahead.

"We mustn't be late. Let's try to go faster."

"Okeh!" Hanna said. "It's pretty hard on this ice, though."

It was; and the street was growing steep. Once Afify stumbled but Hanna picked her up.

"Let's pray," said Afify. "I'll say the Our Father and you say the Hail Mary."

"I don't know it very well," said Hanna. "But I could say the little prayer."

"All right, say that one," said Afify, so they prayed. While Afify said, "Our Father, who art in heaven," Hanna said, "God bless our house. God bless our father and keep him for us." When Afify said, "Hail, Mary, full of grace," Hanna kept on saying, "God bless our house." He said it over and over.

Afify was getting very tired. Hanna's stout little legs seemed as strong as ever. But Afify began to wish she could sit down.

She was getting hungry, too. She remembered that she hadn't eaten any supper. She hadn't even tasted the pastries. The more she remembered how she hadn't eaten, the hungrier she got.

But she was glad she had fasted. Now the Blessed Virgin would help them to get to the park on time. They were coming close to Prospect Park West. She could see the trees rising above the snowy wall. Lights streamed out from the mansions along the boulevard. The broad avenue shone like a mirror.

"Hooray!" cried Hanna. "Now Bobo can skate!" He forgot all Uncle Elias had said about this being a dangerous corner. He ran out on the icy street and slid. And suddenly, all around him, cars honked and screeched and slued. Afify called wildly, but he got back to the sidewalk all right.

"Oh, Hanna!" cried Afify. "Don't you remember that we always stop and wait–"

Hanna interrupted. "I dropped Bobo," he said. His voice was trembling. "We can't leave Bobo out there."

"Of course not," said Afify. And yet–it was almost time now, she was sure, for the Christ Child to be born and the trees to kneel. She shut her eyes tight.

"Please, Blessed Virgin, get us there in time! Please, Blessed Virgin! Hail, Mary, full of grace–"

Afify never gave up. But she felt tears coming. When she opened her eyes, the spears of light thrown by the cars had fuzzy, golden edges. And the street lights had fuzzy diadems. She rubbed her eyes.

"There he is!" Hanna shouted.

"There who is?"

"Bobo! I see him! We can get him when we cross the street."

Oh, thank you Blessed Virgin! Afify thought from her heart. At last the cars stopped coming, and they ran out and

got Bobo, and they crossed, and were soon in the park.

They turned in at the gate with wild animals on top and at first they could not believe their eyes. In the glare from the boulevard, the park was an enchanted garden. It shone with a silvery light.

The fields of snow shone, and the trees shone, and the shrubs. They seemed to have been turned to glass. And she and Hanna had it all to themselves, this crystal wonderland. It was empty. It was silent. It was waiting.

Behind the wall the cars still hurried past, screeching on the icy road. The mansions showed their glowing decorated windows, and there were people inside, of course. But the park was a world apart.

Afify and Hanna looked about, awestruck. Then Afify said gently, "Come! It's almost time."

They quit the path, floundering through the drifts.

The snow was very thick when you broke that gleaming crust. It hugged their legs, and made it hard to walk. But Afify was climbing now in breathless expectation. Nothing would stop her. She knew she would get there.

All around them the glass trees shimmered. And the little glass bushes sparkled with a delicate fire. Every branch and bough, every tiny twig had turned to transparent glass. Where the snow still clung, it wore a coat of glass. Beams of

light danced from tree to tree.

Afify looked up. Stars were twinkling far above. And as she looked the sky seemed to open, going higher and higher. It would show heaven in a moment, she thought.

Their little Secret Place came into view. They pulled harder; and just as they reached it, bells started to ring.

They were not only ringing. They were playing a tune. Grandmother had said that the church bells rang by themselves on the Night of the Birth but she hadn't said they played tunes.

It came upon the midnight clear–

"Hanna! It's midnight!" Afify squeezed his hand and let it go.

"And we've reached the trees!" he said.

They dropped to their knees and blessed themselves.

They shut their eyes and the bells kept on singing.

> *That glorious song of old,*
>
> *From angels bending near the earth*
>
> *To touch their harps of gold–*

Afify opened her wet lashes. And like Grandmother she almost saw the angels. They were coming down from the sky in radiant armies, singing along with the bells. They had white wings and golden hair and floating dresses and rings around their heads.

She and Hanna were just like the shepherds, she thought. They too heard music and saw angels at the Birth, for now, of course, the Christ Child was being born!

She looked up at her three little trees and, sure enough, they were kneeling! Every branch was kneeling, beginning with the lowest and broadest. They bent far down in adoration beneath dazzling crusts of snow. They were fringed with icicles and the icicles, too, swept down. But at the top, tree hands were folded, pointing up to heaven.

Afify was not surprised that they were kneeling.

The majesty of the moment was such that all the world must bow in worship.

> *O come, let us adore him!*
>
> *O come, let us adore him!*

the carols were playing now.

It was one of those moments that you hold in your heart forever.

She looked at Hanna. He was staring upward as raptly as herself.

"We saw them kneeling," she said to him softly.

"Sure," he answered. "Bobo saw them, too."

They knelt for a long time for they were very tired. They were almost too tired to get up. But when at last they struggled to their feet, the little trees still prayed.

They heard afterwards that Father and Mother and Grandmother and Uncle Elias had been frightened, on returning from Mass. For they had found the door open, and they had forgotten that you leave the door open on Christmas Eve.

Father had run to Afify's bed, and Mother had run to Hanna's bed, and Grandmother had sat down in her chair and started saying prayers, and Uncle Elias had looked in the kitchen and under the dining room table.

"I thought you were hiding to see Santa Claus," he explained to Hanna later. "But Santa Claus hadn't even come yet with that sled." (In the morning a fine red sled was under the Christmas tree.)

Before they had had a chance to get too frightened, they heard the door downstairs open and bang. They ran to the landing and saw a little girl and a little boy, covered with snow and dragging their small legs wearily up the stairs.

"Your skirts were hanging out over your snow pants," Mother told Afify. "And Hanna was carrying Bobo by one leg. You looked half dead, but you came to life when you saw us."

Afify remembered that. She had rushed pell-mell to Grandmother.

"They did kneel! They did! Oh, my Grandmother, the trees kneel in Brooklyn, too!"

Father stood very still, and Mother looked at Afify with

a strange expression on her face. She sat down slowly and pulled Hanna into her lap.

"They knelt?" Father asked, sounding bewildered. "Did they, Hanna?"

"Oh, yes, they kneeled all right!" Hanna answered. "No kidding! Bobo saw it, too." He yawned enormously and nestled his head against his mother's breast.

"We didn't see Santa Claus ... but we saw the trees ..."

In the middle of a sentence he fell asleep.

Mother turned to Afify. "What trees, my heart?"

"Why, the trees in the park!"

"Tell us about it, my little love."

Afify glanced around at them excitedly. Her eyes were shining in her little tired face.

"Oh, it was beautiful!" she cried in her chiming voice. "The trees were covered with ice, and they kneeled down and prayed just like they do in Lebanon."

Mother blessed herself. Father blessed himself. Grandmother blessed herself, and looked at Uncle Elias.

He sat down in his straight-backed chair, with his right hand on his right knee, and his left hand on his left knee. But his eyes, beneath the smoky peak of hair, weren't mocking. They looked mistily at Afify.

Mother had caught her now into her arms with Hanna.

And Father was putting his arms around the three.

"Who am I," asked Uncle Elias, "to question how God chooses to perform His miracles?"

And Uncle Elias blessed himself, too.